THIS IS A BORZOI BOOK PUBLISHED BY ALFRED A. KNOPF

Copyright © 2021 by Amanda Driscoll

All rights reserved. Published in the United States by Alfred A. Knopf, an imprint of Random House Children's Books,
a division of Penguin Random House LLC, New York.
Knopf, Borzoi Books, and the colophon are registered trademarks of Penguin Random House LLC.

Visit us on the Web! rhcbooks.com
Educators and librarians, for a variety of teaching tools, visit us at RHTeachersLibrarians.com

Library of Congress Cataloging-in-Publication Data
Names: Driscoll, Amanda, author.
Title: Little Grump Truck / Amanda Driscoll.
Description: First edition. | New York: Alfred A. Knopf Books for Young Readers, 2021. | Audience: Ages 3–6.
Summary: Little Dump Truck is the happiest member of the crew until she has a bad day,
and then her grumpiness affects everyone.
Identifiers: LCCN 2019049883 (print) | LCCN 2019049884 (ebook) | ISBN 978-0-593-30081-7 (hardcover) |
ISBN 978-0-593-30082-4 (lib. bdg.) | ISBN 978-0-593-30083-1 (ebook)
Subjects: CYAC: Cheerfulness—Fiction. | Emotions—Fiction. | Behavior—Fiction. | Dump trucks—Fiction. | Trucks—Fiction.
Classification: LCC PZ7.D7866 Lit 2021 (print) | LCC PZ7.D7866 (ebook) | DDC [E]—dc23
The text of this book is set in 19-point Amasis.
The illustrations were created using pencil sketches painted in Adobe Photoshop.
Book design by Sarah Hokanson

MANUFACTURED IN CHINA
August 2021   10 9 8 7 6 5 4 3 2 1   First Edition
Random House Children's Books supports the First Amendment and celebrates the right to read.

Penguin Random House LLC supports copyright. Copyright fuels creativity, encourages diverse voices, promotes
free speech, and creates a vibrant culture. Thank you for buying an authorized edition of this book and for complying
with copyright laws by not reproducing, scanning, or distributing any part in any form without permission.
You are supporting writers and allowing Penguin Random House to publish books for every reader.

LITTLE GRUMP TRUCK

Amanda Driscoll

Alfred A. Knopf
New York

For my husband, Jack,
who brings me loads of happiness.
—A.D.

Meet Little Dump Truck.

Hello!

She likes hauling,

and dumping,

and dirt pile jumping.

Not so high!

Careful!

Holy moly!

She's the happiest member of the construction crew.

Except when things don't go her way.

When that happens . . .

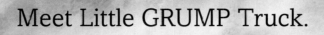

Meet Little GRUMP Truck.

Hurmph.

She doesn't like *anything*.

When Little Grump Truck is in a bad mood, her truck bed fills with grumpies.

They are as heavy as
a hippopotamus, but
not nearly as cute.

The grumpies weigh her down.

She tries to haul.

SO-O-O SLOW.

She tries to dump.

HEAVE HO-O-O.

She tries to jump.

NO GO-O-O.

The crew tries to help.

This only makes her grumpier.

Now the grumpies are as big as a blue whale

and as mean as a T. rex
with a toothache.

Little Grump Truck
says things she would
normally never say.

What do **you** know? You can't even doze a dandelion!

And does things she would
normally never do.

The grumpies grow . . .

And grow . . .

And grow!
Until . . .

Now *everyone* has the grumpies.

Little Grump Truck hangs her head.
She closes her eyes.
The darkness lets her forget the mess.
The quiet helps her focus.

Little Grump Truck feels the earth beneath her tires, the breeze on her windshield, and the sun warming her hood. She hears birds singing, cicadas buzzing, and her own engine humming. She concentrates on these sounds, and her bad day begins to melt away.

Tweedle-tweet-tweet . . .
Her frown relaxes.
Buzzle-buzz-buzz . . .
Her engine cools.
Humm-hummm . . .
Her mind clears and her mood lightens.

When Little DUMP Truck opens her
eyes, the grumpies are gone.

"I'm sorry for losing my cool,"
she says to the crew.

"That's okay," they say.
"It happens sometimes."

Before long, Little
Dump Truck is hauling,

and dumping,

and dirt pile jumping.

She is the happiest member of the crew.